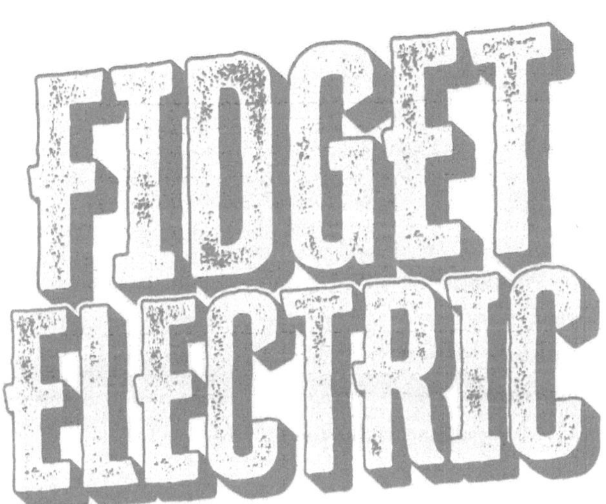

ISBN: 979-8-9889373-9-5

ALSO BY ERIC WILLIFORD

The Dead Ate Cheese

The Big Decay

Rich People $hit

Middle Sister

Frittata

Dedicated to AF and MTW.
Love You

Contents

1. One — 1

2. Two — 4

3. Three — 14

4. Four — 18

5. Five — 22

6. Six — 26

7. Seven — 32

8. Eight — 41

9. Nine — 45

10. Ten — 50

11. Eleven — 55

12. Twelve — 65

13. Thirteen — 67

14. Fourteen — 71

15. Fifteen — 77

16. Sixteen   81

17. Seventeen   86

18. Eighteen   91

19. Nineteen   99

Join My Newsletter   108

Author's Note   109

About the Author   110

— · —

ONE

THE BATHROOM STALL IS covered with graffiti and promises of oral sex.

Crushed Fidget Electric balances on the edge of my maxed-out credit card. It's airy violet with metallic radiations resembling amethyst dust. It gets sucked into a flaring nostril. The burn intensifies. Eyes water. Lightning in powder form.

When you pop a pill, the Fidget hits you in 12 minutes.

They call it running the lights.

When you crush it up and take it through the nose, it hits in 6 minutes.

They call this dusting the lights.

The bathroom reeks of industrial cleaner and pink granular soap. Best to get out before the Fidget hits.

The burger and fries are at the table. Waiting. Timing couldn't be more perfect. My ass slides across the cracked red vinyl-covered foam.

Guy on the fryer has a neck full of prison tats and a face full of grease steam. The air is thick with fry oil, burger sludge, and bacon fat.

You know the Fidget is about to hit when your tongue dries out.

Ice water adds relief as the lights bleed and blur.

The ketchup bottle radiates with the haze of a neon sign. It vibrates in my hand as the glowing redness squirts out of the bottle and forms a puddle on my plate.

Fry after fry gets dipped, then chewed. Salt and acid tap my taste buds. There's ketchup and mustard and mayonnaise and pickles and onion and a slice of tomato on the burger. It still gets dipped in the ketchup before my first bite.

Lines streak across the diner. They zig and zag. Right to left. Up and down. They form squares. Hexagons. Circles. Ovals. My fingers trace the lines and shapes.

"You alright, honey?" Her hair is brown and chopped. Her eyes are tired and glossy. There's a smudge on her apron. Maybe grease? Maybe iced tea? Her manicured fingers slide the check next to the empty plastic cup. She knows there's something wrong with me, but she refills the water anyway.

A hard life full of crazy experiences. In a place like this, half their clientele are users. My eyes focus on the ketchup bottle. "You're gonna need to refill this. Sorry." I hold it up without eye contact.

She grabs it and saunters off. Each step echoes between my ears.

Another dip of the burger. Another bite. Another fry goes into the ketchup. Then into my mouth.

The front door opens, and sunlight floods the diner, causing me to squint. Two cops march in with bodies that make you question the academy's standards. We make eye contact for a moment. Then my focus shifts to the check on the table.

They stare at me until they heave themselves into the stools at the counter.

My phone vibrates and glows through the pocket. Time to go. I leave a twenty on the $10 check. The booth hisses as the air compresses as I slide out, careful to not attract the attention of the cops.

Across the street from the diner sits a black cargo van. It's the type of van you get when you're up to no good. When I'm within two feet of it, the engine roars to life and the door slides open.

I hop in and the door slams shut behind me.

— · —

Two

THEY STILL CALL ME New Guy.

And they don't tell the new guy where we're going or what we're doing. But everyone else in the van is grabbing shotguns, handguns, and automatic assault rifles out of the duffel bags in the middle of the floor.

Never one to be left out, I grab a pair of 9MM's. Polymer frames gleaming matte black. Scratched off serial numbers. Wear and tear on the sides of both guns.

All around me, the cast of characters examine their weapons. Pecan, with the maniacal gleam in his eye, loads a shotgun. Dillo, his younger brother with the three-day old black eye, slams a clip into an assault rifle.

In addition to the two brothers, there's five others, not including myself. There's a driver whipping the van into every pothole the road has to offer. There's a group of crooks and cutthroats who I've never met before. Green Mohawk loads a sawed-off shotgun. Face Tat's slides a magazine into place with a snap. Blue Beard rests an Uzi in his lap, closes his eyes, and leans back against the quaking van.

At the front of the van sits the lone female, Ve. Pink-streaked ponytailed hair. Machete on the hip. Sawed-off shotgun in hand.

Fingers slide rounds into stacks with a whoosh.

Magazines find their homes and snap into place.

Dry brass rattles like coins in a tin.

Ve grumbles loud enough for everyone to hear. "These fuckers are putting fake shit on the streets. Broadway wants us to remind them, and everyone else, we're the only ones bringing Fidget Electric to the streets."

Our target must be a lab or stash house.

This was bound to happen. Ever since Pecan found the kid slinging fake violet, the crew has been frothing at the mouth.

Dillo unzips a duffel bag full of clown masks. The creepy smiling mask goes to Pecan. Ve gets a jester clown mask.

I get the clown with the droopy melted face.

The windowless van keeps our identities secret from the outside world. It also keeps the outside world a secret from us.

Ve says, "This is a biker club. One percenters. They'll be armed. Heads on swivels."

The van stops.

Ve says, "Masks on, boys."

We put our masks on.

Ve opens the back door. Jumps out of the van. Breaks into a full sprint towards the house.

We spill out of the van into a lower middle-class neighborhood. Single family homes. Cars on cinderblocks. Fried lawns.

Midday warmth coaxes sweat from my pores. Sun rays blind my already obscured vision.

The mask smells of cheap plastic. My breath is hot with ketchup and anticipation.

Ve blows the door open with a shotgun blast.

We rush into a house full of screams.

There's a table with scales. Baggies. Mountains of violet pills.

Behind the table are women of all shapes, sizes, and skin colors. Dressed in only their panties. They cower and duck.

Another shotgun blast from Ve sends some sap in a leather jacket hurling back into the hallway.

A handgun splits the room into shimmering echoes. Topless women flee.

Exit wounds explode out of the women, leaving behind little volcanoes of erupting blood.

Pecan and Dillo rake pills into duffle bags.

Motorcycles approach. Their roar rattles the drywall.

Down the hall, the bathroom door opens and out steps another leather-jacket-clad, scraggly-haired one percenter. My gun cracks. The pop stretches like taffy.

His blood dots the wall behind him.

Gunpowder tastes sweet and metallic.

Shots ring out all around. From outside. And inside. Dillo flips the table. I take cover with him and his brother.

Walls breathe. Paint pulsates with the rhythm of the shots.

A gruff voice from the door yells, "There must be two dozen of them."

Machine guns rattle. Each round a tiny waterfall cascading into brass.

Ve stands and pumps her shotgun.

The remaining women hit the floor and cover their ears.

Face Tats, Mohawk, and Blue Beard head outside with guns blazing. Ve follows them out.

Someone steals a glance through the window. My hand squeezes. Glass shatters. The head snaps backwards and out of sight.

Gotta get to the van. I crouch and sprint out the front door and into a war zone.

Our van is ablaze. Orange and yellow licking the sky. The driver gets out. Body on fire. Falls to his knees. Bullets jolt his body until it falls. The corpse burns.

The one percenters are everywhere. They race behind the neighbors' houses. Take cover behind parked cars. Drive their motorcycles across yards. One hand steering, the other unloading rounds.

A monarch butterfly hovers into view. It grows larger and larger with each flap of its wings.

This butterfly is the real enemy. It must be destroyed. If we're not careful, this thing will grow big enough to consume us all. I take aim, but the butterfly smiles. Ready to meet death.

Police sirens wail, confirming what the pit of my stomach has been telling me.

Coming out the front was a terrible idea.

The cops are roughly a quarter mile from us.

Ve remains in the middle of the street, chopping down bikers with shotgun shells.

The butterfly will live for now. Bullets whizz all around me. Sirens grow louder.

Pecan greets me at the front door to the house. "Where you going, New Guy?"

I say, "Cops." And brush past him into the house.

Inside the house, a handgun snaps, echoing into tiny explosions. Dillo is on the floor. Blood evacuating through the hole in his leg. My eyes trace up and see a young woman raising her gun to finish him.

Instincts kick in. My handgun barks. First bullet tags her shoulder. The woman spins and tries to raise her gun, but can't. Another bullet leaves a hole in her neck. She drops the gun. Then her body collapses.

Behind me, Pecan yells, "You alright, Dillo?"

Dillo pushes the bag across the floor. "Take it."

Pecan grabs the bag and eyes me.

I make my way to Pecan's brother. "I'll take Dillo out the back." I don't wait for a response. I get Dillo to his feet. Drape an arm over my shoulder and drag him through the kitchen and out the back door.

Sounds of death and gunfire fill the air from the front yard. Above us, a helicopter circles the neighborhood.

Dillo says, "Fucker almost shot me in my ass."

Trees form a natural fence that gives way to a steep hill. We stumble down the hill and into a pile of leaves and rocks.

On the other side of the woods is a street.

We traverse the sticks and rocks and roots and leaves and dirt until we reach the street. Sirens and gunshots are all around us.

On both sides of the street are gas stations. Run down restaurants and sandwich shops. A pawn shop and liquor store. Quickie marts and check cashers.

We ditch the masks into a trash can.

People scream.

Horns honk.

The violence from the neighborhood expands like a plume of smoke.

The low, hot rumble of a motorcycle violates the air. About a block up, a one percenter heads straight for us.

A bell over the convenience store door signals our arrival. The store's owner, a bald Middle Eastern man, raises his hands and shouts, "No trouble. No trouble."

I shove Dillo to the floor in front of the counter and hit the floor next to him.

The bike approaches. Air shudders. A coughing god clearing his throat. And then it stops.

The guy behind the counter pleads. "I don't want any trouble. Please—"

A boom and glass shatters. The bald man gasps. Wind sneaks in through the closed door. Behind the breeze enters a bald man with a Santa Claus beard and a leather jacket.

He doesn't think to look down.

I roll, aim, and shoot in one furious motion. My clip unloads, peppering the bearded biker's torso, stomach, and groin.

In an instant, I'm on my feet. The biker sucks in his last few breaths.

Dillo says, "We gotta move."

Behind the counter, the store owner clutches his ribs. Blood seeps between his fingers. The red on his shirt widens by the second. Eyes full of fear. "Help me."

A roll of paper towels sits under the cash register. I grab it and press it against the hole in his ribs.

Dillo says, "Fuck this guy. Let's go."

The store owner whimpers. "You can't leave me."

I apply pressure to the wound with the paper towel roll. "Keep pressure on this."

A gun cocks. Dillo says, "Ever been to prison, New Guy?"

My heart rate spikes. Instinct tells me the gun is pointed at my head. "Just county."

Dillow says, "Toughest thing about prison is falling asleep when all you hear is rape and grown men crying."

"If we leave him here, he'll die."

"No more sleepless nights, my man."

I say, "Okay. We leave." I let go of the paper towel roll. "Keep pressure on that." When I turn to face Dillo, he puts his gun back in his pants. I drape his arm back around my shoulder and we head for the door.

The double tap stutters. First shot melts into the second. His shirt dampens mine. His smirk is demonic. My truth. His last thought. Words want to come out but can't. Teeth stained red.

"No more sleepless nights, Dillo." I step away. Dropping him to the floor. His body twitches. The red pool underneath him grows and morphs. Shapes come and go. Circles. Squares. A butterfly.

"Please don't kill me." The store owner's eyes dart from shelf to shelf.

I arrive next to him and kneel down. Metallic notes ding as I punch the number into my cell. Before the voice on the other end can say anything, the words pour out of me. "This is Officer 5365, requesting an ambulance to the corner of 5th and Warren. I've got a civilian with a bullet wound and two others fatally wounded. In the convenience store. Hurry."

Relief washes over the store owner.

My eyes dig into the man's soul. "I have to leave you. If the wrong person comes in here, they'll kill us both."

"Please. There could be more of them."

"Stay down. And don't tell anyone what happened here. If anyone finds out I shot that guy, I'll kill you myself." I step over Dillo and the bearded biker and exit the store.

Guns sputter at half the frequency of before. Screams still pierce the air. More than anything, the air is full of sirens and cops barking orders into megaphones.

Even the helicopter is gone.

A cop car hurls down the street towards me. The windshield is punctured and the hood is covered in blood.

Scenarios play out in my head. If this is a cop, it could be trouble.

My hand moves to the gun on my hip. Eyes narrow. Through the shattered glass, something seems off.

Is that pink hair?

The cop car screeches to a halt. The driver's side door flings open. My gun raises.

A woman steps out in a SWAT team helmet. The outfit is familiar. Pink locks flow out the bottom of the helmet and rest on her shoulders. She pulls the helmet off.

It's Ve.

My weapon lowers.

Ve says, "Get in."

I do as I'm told.

THREE

Gunfire lives in my ears. *Pop-pop-pop.*

My apartment is a dump. A place to lay my head in a rare moment of silence. Dirty dishes cover the counter. Crushed soda cans cover the floor. Little land mines of jagged aluminum ready to cut holes in my feet. Half of them I don't remember drinking.

Echoes crawl down my spine like static. Blinds half shut. Sun rays slice through like thin blades, dicing the room. My hands won't stop shaking. One pill gets dumped onto the coffee table. I use a spoon to crush it into powder. Roll up a dollar. It feels like ritual. Or punishment.

Crush it. Line it. Snort it.

Mouth tastes like metal. Sweat stings my eyes. Dillo's blood stains my jeans and shirt.

The fridge hums like a threat. The radiator knocks like a door.

If the cashier listened, he would have made it. If he was feeling bold, he might be dead. If the crew finds out what happened, they'll come here.

Waiting for a knock that could mean my death.

Fleeing crosses my mind. But running only leads to more running. Eventually you run out of breath. Your legs give out. The thing you're running from never picks up its pace. It chases you with patience. Quiet. Plodding. Lurking around every corner. The threats are everywhere and nowhere. It could be tomorrow. It could be twenty years from now.

Not knowing is the reason you don't run.

Sirens slide past the building. Close, then distant. With any luck, they'll come for me. End this charade. Being lost within myself is no way to live. Yesterday's me is not today's me.

Fidget Electric tells me to ignore the spiral.

Be happy you survived.

Trust they don't know the truth.

The powder sits at the bottom of my stomach like sand. A steady, humming pressure radiates up my spine. Under the shower, the water hits me like a drum roll. Hard and clean. Steam climbs. Light from overhead glistens the tiles. The glass fogs. The room breathes.

The water is too hot, and I love that it's too hot. It burns along the ridge of my shoulders. Sharp, polite knives. My hands move clumsy and expert at once. Soap, scrub, rinse.

Each drop rings as if struck by a tiny bell.

Ping, ping, ping.

Sound painted violet.

My skin maps little lightning lines, traced by a finger, and the tracks glow for a half second. Light folds back into the steam.

Shampoo lather feels like snow in my palms. It swims with flecks of violet when I lift my head. Tiny metallic sparks swirl in the suds and spiral down my arms.

In the bedroom, my wet nakedness relaxes my muscles. Water evaporates off me with a dull vibration before disappearing into the room. Too wet to sit or lay on the bed, I stand in the middle of the room with the fan on. Senses alive and alert. I can feel the city expand and contract with each honked horn and police siren and ambulance and shout and flicker of a traffic light.

I am the bleeding heart of the city.

Someone pounds on the front door. More violent than a knock.

The city leaves me, and I fish the gun out from under the pillow.

The something pounds on the door again.

Person or beast, I can't tell.

But it wants in. Whatever it is.

Gun raised, I make it to the front door. "Hello?"

No answer.

Through the peephole, the hall is empty.

I say, "I'm not in the mood for your games."

The floor shakes beneath me. Something is pounding from downstairs. It rattles the walls. Then it's on top of me. More pounding. The floors and ceiling give, ready to crumble under the stress of the assault.

I point my gun up and down and up and down. Ready to put a bullet into whoever, or whatever is trying to get in. Every bit of me wants to fire a warning shot, let them know what will happen if they break through.

But if I discharge my weapon, and there's no body to show for it, there will be questions I can't answer.

I can't shoot until it reveals itself.

The pounding grows in force. Louder. More violent. But nothing comes through.

Fidget Electric tells me to get dressed. It tells me to flee while I still can.

— · —

FOUR

Children laugh.

It's enough to wake me in pieces. Twitch here. A sigh. My eyes crack open and flood my vision with the brightness of a million high noons.

The kids argue. One has something the other one wants.

Across me is a camper. Brother and sister, both under ten, chase each other with bubble guns. Shock brings me into an upright position.

I'm behind the steering wheel in my car. At a rest stop on the side of some highway.

Fidget Electric brought me here and I'm not sure how long ago that was.

My phone tells me it's 6:37 Wednesday morning.

Shit.

I need to meet Naomi at her office at eight.

The car wakes with a groggy grumble.

Back on the highway. The GPS says it should only take an hour. My throat is dry and my stomach is empty. My blood feels like it's flowing in the wrong direction. Breakfast will have to be a couple bottles of water and a gas station donut.

The traffic back into the city is unrelenting. Gridlock and angry drivers. Two different accidents grind things to a halt, but there's still enough time for me to grab breakfast before the meeting with Naomi.

In the parking lot of the glass monstrosity of an office building, I'm shoveling entire powdered donuts into my mouth. After three bottles of water, the powdered donuts have dried my mouth out even more. The fourth bottle of water gets chugged and discarded into the back seat with all the others.

Office drones pass my car and the few who dare a glance into my car quickly turn away from the powdered crazy person with the wild eyes. Nobody wants to know what the strange, bugged out man is doing.

Until Naomi.

She sees me, and with her pregnant girl waddle, makes her way over. Eyes red and frantic. She hasn't slept and I already know why. She lets herself into the passenger side.

I don't know why, but I silently offer her my last donut. She waves it off like it's a poisoned apple.

She says, "You look like shit."

"I feel worse." The last powdered donut gets crammed into my mouth.

She says, "Were you involved in that shootout yesterday? It's been all over the news."

I'm out of water and my mouth is a desert. My tongue separates the donut into sections so words will have a pathway to get out. "I can't tell you details of the operation."

She says, "I thought this was only supposed to be a few weeks. You said it was only going to be a— What did you call it?"

"A buy bust."

"It's been months, Max. Months." She sighs in her special way of telling me she's more disappointed than angry.

I say, "It'll be over soon. I promise." My fingers drum the steering wheel, leaving white powder residue. I'm failing the sobriety test.

She asks, "What are you on?"

"I'm not sleeping real well."

She says, "Whatever you're on, promise me you'll get off it."

"I promise."

Her body leans towards me and she sticks her face inches from mine. "Promise me again."

"I promise."

She opens the door and heaves herself around. With her legs out the door, and her body in the car but turned away from me, she says, "It's going to be hard for us to have a family if you're dead."

FIVE

My stomach is a bottomless pit.

Bowling alley fried onion rings help to fill it momentarily. They aren't the best onion rings, but they're greasy, and after being drenched in ranch, they're slightly better than terrible.

This is the ideal place to meet. It's sad. The lighting is low and it's on the outskirts of town. There's no reason anyone should recognize me.

Most importantly, the crew has their own run-down bowling alley they frequent on the opposite side of the city. Coming here would be considered a sign of disrespect.

Even with that said, I sit facing the front door. If I'm going to die in a derelict bowling alley, I want to see it coming.

The beer isn't ice cold, but it's not hot, so there's that. It's a light beer, and it calms my nerves just enough to help me gather my thoughts.

I need out of this operation. It's worse than I imagined. Fidget Electric. Shootouts. Paranoia. Sweats. Bar fights.

It's all way more than I signed up for. At this pace, I may not see next week.

Reid enters the bowling alley. Patchy grey beard and clothes in need of a wash. He's been on the force so long nobody remembers how he got the limp. With more effort than it should take, my handler finally gets into the chair across from me. He eyes my onion rings, so I push the basket towards him. In one fluid motion, he scoops up the two biggest rings and stuffs them into his pie hole. Between chews, he says, "We got the surveillance video from the convenience store. You're in the clear."

I drown an onion ring in ranch, stick it in my mouth and chew.

He says, "The store owner won't mention you. I saw him myself to be sure."

Fidget Electric drags me into a pool of dehydration and exhaustion. My knees shake with nerves. The blood in my veins boils. There's a pill in my pocket. A quick trip to the bathroom will get me right. If I were smart, I would have crushed it before he got here, but the bathroom in this place has got to be filthy. More reason to hold out until I can get into my car.

Reid says, "That shoot out left a lot of people dead. Some of them cops. Some of them regular folks caught in the crossfire."

My wife wants me off Fidget Electric. Getting off this job is the only way to kick it. I need it to deal with this crew of crazies. It's the only way I can lose myself and not live in fear of what these people will have me do next.

Fidget Electric is how I'm surviving.

But promises were made.

Reid eyes every empty table around us, then leans towards me. "You're on it, aren't you?"

It's not the most groundbreaking statement. I'm shaking. My eyes are bloodshot and my clothes are wrinkled from sleeping in my car. This body of mine was surging, and now it's crashing. I gulp down my beer.

Reid says, "You gotta keep it together."

I down half of what's left and use the back of my sleeve to wipe the room temperature beer off my lips.

Reid grabs the last onion ring. "Have you met Broadway yet?"

I say, "This was supposed to be a buy bust."

He says, "I know. But an opportunity presented itself. You took advantage. It's what makes you so great at this."

"You gotta get me out."

Reid takes the entire onion ring in one bite. The chewing is slow and methodical. A man with nothing but time enjoying someone else's food. "We need you to deliver the head of the snake. If we pull you out without taking this crew down, you'll be running the rest of your life."

"You telling me I gotta keep running around the city, having shootouts with one percenters until, what, I get a meeting with a guy we're not even sure exists?"

Reid reaches into the inside of his coat, pulls out a folded manilla folder, and slides it across the table.

I say, "What's this?"

Instead of answering, Reid dips his finger in the ranch and sucks it off.

Inside the folder is a recording device. Anger wells inside me. It takes every ounce of restraint I can muster to not yell across the table. "You want me to wear a wire?"

"If you can't get a meeting with Broadway, get one of them on tape saying something incriminating. We can offer a deal, get them to flip. Then you're out of this mess."

I say, "If they catch me wearing this, I'm dead on the spot. You know that, right?"

"You want out, this is the quickest way."

— • —

Six

Seated behind the steering wheel in my parked Honda Civic and crushing a violet pill on the driver's manual is a balancing act I'm not proud of.

Promises were made.

Crush it. Line it. Snort it.

Fidget Electric is the reason I get out of the car. Fidget Electric is the reason I march into the diner.

Pecan has already commandeered a booth. He snarls at an exhausted waitress. "What the fuck am I supposed to do with four pieces of bacon?" He deconstructs the BLT on his plate. "Bring me at least four more pieces."

I slide into the booth as he slaps the waitress's ass when she turns to leave. He plucks a tot off his plate and holds it up. "Tot?"

I wave him off.

He shrugs his shoulders and tosses it in his mouth. "Your loss. Crunchy on the outside. Soft on the inside.

Sorta like that waitress." His laugh erupts louder than necessary.

An hour ago, they called and told me to meet here. They didn't mention Pecan. They didn't tell me why I needed to come here. Considering the timing, this feels like a trap. A glance over my shoulder reveals nothing out of the ordinary.

Pecan laughs. "You seem nervous, New Guy."

"You got any idea what this job is?"

"Nope."

The waitress arrives and drops a plate of bacon in front of Pecan. He eyes her and grins. "Was that so hard?"

Without a word, she marches to her other table.

Pecan re-constructs his sandwich. "The lost art of customer service." He smashes the top down on the bacon and it crunches. "You seem jumpy. Get yourself a tea. It's not sweet tea, but if you dump enough sugar in it, it's passable."

"I don't think sugar is the answer."

He takes a monstrous bite of his BLT. Mid chew he says, "Back when I lived in San Antonio, I used to run with this crew. There was this guy. Called himself Jericho. He used to tell everybody about how crazy he was. Always had a story to prove it. Funny thing is, crazy people never call themselves crazy. They think they're normal. That's what makes them crazy. See what I'm saying? Anyway, this guy, Jericho—"

Both of our phones vibrate. I glance at mine and say, "We got five minutes."

He checks his phone and places it face down on the table. "So this guy, Jericho, always finds a way to get out of doing jobs with us. He's never around when a fight breaks out. I start asking myself, *What's up with Jericho?*" Another bite. This one takes out about half the remaining BLT. He chews with patience, as if he's not in the middle of a story. He washes it down with his tea. "One day, I decided to follow him. I see him meet with some old guy in a cheap suit. Come to find out, crazy Jericho was an undercover cop." He crams the rest of the sandwich into his mouth.

Fidget Electric tells me to shoot him on the spot. Or run. This is a trap and I walked right into it. Pecan chews and stares at me and chews some more. He washes the sandwich down with a thirty second sip from his straw. His eyes never leave me.

I say, "What's the point, Pecan?"

Pecan continues. "We had been pulling jobs in a bunch of different counties, so we weren't sure which precinct Jericho was from. To cover our bases, we sent pieces of Crazy Jericho to all the departments within a forty-mile radius. A hand went to Medina. The torso went to Kendall. We sent his head to Gillespie."

I lean back in my chair for easier access to my gun. "You accusing me of something?"

Pecan tosses three tater tots into his mouth. One after the other. "Just trying to impress you with a story about how perfectly normal I am." He tosses a twenty onto the table. "I don't need change, let's get."

The sedan is so old you have to use a crank to roll the windows down. Ve drives. It's the first time I've seen her since she picked me up in the cop car. Pecan sits next to her. I'm the new guy, so I'm in the back. All the windows are down, and the air swirls through the car like a little tornado. The light is blinding and there's no music. We ride in silence and all I want to do is open the door and jump out.

Buildings give way to trees. Highways become two-lane roads. In the city, there were bus stops and pedestrians in suits. Now there's nothing but grass and roadkill. After an hour of unbearable silence, I ask, "Anybody wanna tell me where we're going?"

Pecan says, "Damn, New Guy. You're on the clock, so you're getting paid. Enjoy the ride." He turns to Ve and snarls. "He's the jumpy type."

Ve says, "I've noticed."

My legs go liquid. Teeth grind. Goosebumps populate my forearm. The sedan glides past a deer carcass. "If this job is anything like the last one, I'll need to swing by my place and grab a few grenades."

Pecan says, "He's also a comedian."

Ve says, "Ha ha, New Guy."

Sweat dampens the back of my shirt. "Guessing this one is for Broadway?"

Ve says, "We only work for Broadway."

Pecan turns to face me. "You sure ask a lot of questions, New Guy."

"The last job nearly got me killed, so yeah. I'm a bit curious."

Pecan whips back around so he's facing forward. "Last job got my brother killed. Count your blessings."

Ve faces the road. Her focus is intense. "Five grand each. At max, two days' work."

Pecan says, "Damn."

I shift in the back seat. The old, cracked leather is sticky and the entire car reeks of decades old cigarettes and mildew. "Doing what?"

Ve snaps off the answer. She's already bored with me. "Babysitting."

Pecan stiffens. "I ain't tryin' to watch no damn kids."

Ve continues to focus on driving. "I know you're tough and all, Pecan, but try not to murder the English language. Some of us want to continue using it."

SEVEN

THE CAR PULLS INTO a clearing and there's already a tinted black sedan in front of the place. We get out and I take in the area. Ve grabs a duffel bag out of the trunk.

It sits like it's thinking. The cabin. Half-swallowed by the trees. Half-spat out by fog.

Boards the color of old bark doused in rainwater. Slick and grey and slimy green. The forest decided to grow a house but got bored halfway through. Everything around it hums with a low electrical breath from the moss and the wet ground and the sky about to storm.

The porch sags forward. A tired grin. Nails poke out like broken teeth. A single chair, tipped just wrong. Invisible wind rocks it. Shadows under the porch pulse in rhythm with my heartbeat.

The wood smells wet and alive. A throat right before a cough. Windows are blind. Glazed over with grime. Inside are little flickers of violet light. The powder in my system whispers that it's a reflection. My blood tells me it's something looking back.

The trees lean close. Patiently waiting. Branches sway. Slow and synchronized, either they breathe with me, or I breathe with them. The forest hides its noise in the spaces between brush and grass. Limbs and leaves. Every sound has a tail. Drips echo twice. The breeze offers treacherous secrets.

The air is charged metallic. A world plugged in, and this cabin is the socket. My tongue tastes like static, violet-bright and electric-sweet. I refuse to touch the porch rail. It wants to hum under my hand and whisper my name through the wood grain.

This place isn't empty. It's paused. Waiting for someone to press play again.

The door flies open. A tired man in a crisp black suit with a black tie and a white shirt bounds out of the cabin. Fury in his eyes and intention in his stride. "You pay me to transport the goods, not to sit around and wait."

Pecan is already reaching for his gun.

Ve's voice soothes the situation. Each word both apology and threat. "We appreciate your patience. I trust everything is in order?"

The guy in the suit says, "It is."

Ve pulls an envelope from her back pocket. "Then this is for you." When the driver grabs the envelope, Ve pulls him in close and whispers, "We enjoy your service, don't force me to terminate you." She releases the envelope and the angry driver shuffles back to his black sedan, gets in, and speeds away.

Pecan takes his hand off the gun.

Ve says, "There should be three shipping containers."

The inside of the cabin inhales when we step in. The air's wet and sweet and rotten. Smells like rain and old teeth.

Walls sweat and its paper peels in curls. Mold creeps like veins. Black and green and reaching.

Heads everywhere. Dead faces nailed to the walls. Elk. Wolf. Bear. Their eyes gleam. Glass with a pulse behind it. I move, they follow. Tiny flicks of violet inside the sockets. I blink. The elk winks back.

The floor moans with every step. A warning declared in rhythm under my shoes. It's breathing me in.

There's a chair in the corner, slouched and damp. Looks like it's been waiting too long. Leather cracked like dry lips. Feels like it's whispering, *sit, just sit, you'll see.*

The fireplace is sick with moss growing through brick, a half-burned log sags into itself. Above it, a painting of a hunter, face melted with mold. His mouth gone. His eyes gleam violet when I breathe.

Something hums. Not a machine. Not alive. Wires of light crawl from antler to antler, dust lit like crushed stars. I wave my hand. The air moves like glowing water.

A crow sits on the gun rack. Feathers cracked, eyes black as holes. The guns shine clean and not clean. They smell like iron rain.

I blink and the walls shift. The heads blink back. The whole cabin creaks like it's waking up with a polite hunger. *Please may I have some toast?*

I can taste the air. Mildew and sadness bathed in violet. It coats my tongue like battery acid, sweet at the edges but still deadly.

Everything leans toward me. The cabin's waiting for something. Maybe me. Maybe not. I take a step back. The walls lean closer.

It smells like the inside of an animal. No wonder the driver wanted to get the hell out of here. It's been twenty seconds and I'm already desperate to leave.

The shipping containers are on the couch. They sit close together. Three shapes of fear breathing the same damp air. The cabin lights are low; the walls hum in electric ribbons.

The youngest can't be more than twenty-five. Grey hoodie over an elastic waist long blue skirt. Skin so pale it looks borrowed from the moon. Her face is blotched pink, fever spots high on the cheeks, eyes glassy. She's either coming down from something or been crying for hours. Her hair's wheat-colored and limp with humidity. When she exhales, it sounds like tissue paper tearing. I want to hand her a blanket or whatever calm I can muster.

Next to her, the older one. Forty something. Heavy with loose fitting sweatpants the color of ash. She rocks in small, angry movements. Her shaved sides glint under the lamplight; the longer hair on top sticks out like it's trying to escape her skull. Her skin's flushed, a hot pink against the gray fabric. Every few seconds she wipes her palms on her thighs, leaving dark blooms in the fabric like bruises.

Perched on the edge of the cushion is the girl in the flowered sundress. Knees together, hands folded like she's bracing for news. Her eyes are soft brown, wide, fragile. There's a tremor in her jaw she's pretending not to have. The sundress belongs somewhere warmer. Somewhere that doesn't smell like mildew and static.

The room swims. Air glows violet around them. Three figures wrapped in the same anxious filament. The couch groans under their weight but doesn't protest. They look like people who came too far to end up here, and the cabin seems to know it. The mounted heads on the walls tilt their glass eyes away, embarrassed.

The women don't talk. They just breathe in unison, small clouds of fear and fatigue. The youngest's lips move, maybe counting, maybe praying. The older woman clenches her jaw and stares at the window. The one in the sundress watches them both, waiting for a cue that never comes.

I should say something kind, but the words melt on my tongue. The air is thick with moisture and empathy. The electric hum carries on, steady and endless.

Ve drops her bag on the floor and steps forward. Without a word, she commands the room. "You speak English?"

The women on the couch glance at each other and nod.

Ve says, "Good. I don't care if you get hungry, thirsty, or tired. All I care about is getting my pills out of your stomachs." She bends over and unzips the duffel bag. "Which one of you is Lotte?"

The older woman raises her hand.

Ve pulls a bottle of laxatives out of the bag. "You should have eighty, correct?"

The woman nods.

Ve fishes in her bag for something unseen. "That means you two have sixty each." She pulls out a tube of toothpaste and a bottle of mouthwash. "Okay Lotte, take the other two into the bathroom and show them how to do it. My pellets better be clean when you bring them out."

Lotte takes the three items from Ve and leads the other two women into the bathroom down the hall.

For the first time all day, my muscles relax. Maybe this isn't a trap. I take a seat at the kitchen table and allow myself to exhale. On some level, they've accepted me. Even given me another job. What started as the day I thought I was going to die could become the day I need to get out of this mess.

Pecan grabs a bottle of whiskey out of the cupboard and takes an epic swig.

I say, "What is this place?"

Pecan glares at me. Confused. "What does it look like?"

"I know it's a cabin. Who owns it?" I try to appear relaxed. Fool him into thinking this is nothing more than small talk.

"Broadway owns it." He offers me the bottle. I accept and gulp it down. Not as epic as his, but enough to persuade him to lower his guard.

I hand the bottle back to him and say, "How long you think this is gonna take?"

Pecan takes another swig. "They gotta shit out two-hundred balloons between the three of them. Get comfortable."

"New Guy!" Ve beckons from the main room, her voice sharp and commanding. "Make yourself useful."

When I arrive, she hands me a Ziploc bag of green and a few zig-zags. The duffel bag is full of handguns, an assault rifle, and an Uzi. I motion to the arsenal. "I thought this wasn't that type of job."

Ve says, "They need cleaning. And I need something to occupy my time."

I take a seat on the couch and get to work.

Ve takes a nine out of the bag and disassembles it. With her attention on the gun, she asks, "Got a girlfriend, New Guy?"

"No."

"Hot piece like you? I figured girls would be stuffing their panties in your mailbox."

The green is broken up and ready to be sprinkled onto the paper. "That what you do? Stuff your panties in mailboxes?"

Ve says, "I club them over the head and drag them into my cave."

"How romantic." I roll the joint.

"Romance leads to relationships. Solitude is more my flavor."

I lick the joint to seal the deal. "Solitude leads to dying with thirty-seven cats."

Ve blows through the barrel of the handgun before taking a brush to the inside. "Cats don't plot on you while you sleep."

"You've never lived with a cat, have you?" I offer her the freshly rolled joint.

"Get a lighter." She struts to the front door.

— · —

EIGHT

Searching the drawers for a lighter when Pecan sidles up next to me.

"I got dibs on the one in the sundress." The gleam in his eye tells me he's not talking about dinner and a movie.

I say, "She's not a blue-ribbon cow."

"The hell she isn't. As soon as she's empty, I'm gonna fill her back up."

All I want is to find a damn lighter and be done with this. "She may not want you to fill her up."

"Who says it's up to her?"

Mercifully, I find a lighter behind a bag of rubber bands and make my escape. Part of me wants to stay, make sure Pecan doesn't do something to force my hand.

Like his brother Dillo.

Outside and the air is crisp. Ve's seated on the steps in front of the cabin. Her gaze is distant. She's either exhausted or strategizing something devious. It's impossible to tell. I take a seat next to her, offer both the lighter and the joint. She accepts. The joint crackles like a fuse when she lights it. Tiny sparks crawl up the paper, orange turning gold, gold turning brown at the edges.

She passes it back to me and I take a drag. It knows what I've got in my veins. Smoke hits my tongue like an ex-lover. Bitter and familiar, all ozone and burnt sugar. It slides down my throat and wafts behind my eyes.

I exhale and the smoke comes out silver, almost singing, curling like cursive in the air.

For a second I taste everything: pine, ash, battery metal, something floral that isn't there. My teeth tingle. The joint glows brighter than it should, like it's watching me.

Or I'm watching it watch me.

I pass it back to my boss.

She accepts it. Stares at the tiny embers on the end. "You handled yourself pretty well with the bikers."

A compliment, and I'm not sure how to take it. Is she being nice? Or is there an endgame at play? Soothe me with kind words, then when my guard is down, she slithers in a kill shot. I play it cool. See where this is headed. "Thanks."

Smoke exits her mouth and she studies the plume. This woman and her dramatic pauses. She's dancing around the ring, deciding where to land her next jab. Will she soften me up with another compliment? A body blow to hurt my defenses. Or is it time to reveal what she knows about me? An uppercut to put me out of my misery.

Ve says, "What do they say about me when I'm not around?"

Is she being genuine? Could it be this pink haired psychopath is in need of a friend? I take the joint from her. Before it reaches my lips, I study her for what could have been five seconds or five minutes. Finally, the words come. "Why do you care?"

"I don't."

"But you're asking."

Ve watches me take a pull from the joint. It's almost gone. Only enough for each of us to have one more drag. "Does it involve the "B" word?" She accepts the joint with a laugh both genuine and melancholy."

"I may have heard one or two people say it. But they meant it in a good way. Like, you know, don't fuck with Ve. She's a crazy bitch."

"And in your eyes, that's a positive?"

This is a test. Maybe a loyalty test. Maybe something deeper. This woman isn't confiding in me. She's peeling layers to see what's underneath. "Considering our line of work, yeah."

She hands the J back to me. "You have no idea what I've had to do just to get these douche bags to respect me."

"I can only imagine." The joint is done. My shoe grinds it into the ground. Ve's eyes burrow into the side of my face. She either wants to kill me or fuck me. It takes everything in me to not return the gaze and find out which. My eyes remain straight ahead while my brain mulls over what's going on inside me.

Powder. Whiskey. Weed.

All battling for supremacy.

Ve stands and glares down at me. "I plant the seed of fear and over time it blossoms into respect." She opens the door to the cabin. "Break's over."

— · —

NINE

Staring at the oven until one of us blinks.

Thoughts appear in calligraphy and dissipate seconds later. Whiskey warms my insides. Weed slows the world around me. Fidget Electric warps reality.

Questions breeze by in a sprint. Explanations run in place. Brainwaves fire at blistering speeds with no destination.

Do these people know who I am? If they brought me here to kill me, there's no point in waiting it out. They could have shot me when we pulled up. My corpse should be six feet in the earth.

The only logical explanation is that they don't know how they feel about me. I'm on this job because they need a verdict. Kill him or embrace him.

Are they on the same page? Or is one convinced I'm not who I claim, and this gig is their chance to convince the other.

Pecan told me the story at the diner as a warning. Did I tip my hand? Give him the ammo he needs to go to Ve? No. I played it the only way I could. Any criminal would be pissed at being called a cop. I'm not sure I remember the entire conversation. Something could have slipped out. Given him the evidence he needs to rat me out and leave my corpse in the woods.

"Are you...crying?" The voice is soft with a staccato that confirms English is her second language.

My hands wipe under my eyes, and sure enough, they're wet. Fuck. I am crying. Why am I standing in the kitchen crying? Fuck. "No. Umm." Desperate, my eyes latch on to her hand clutching the freezer bag stuffed with pellets. Her name scribbled across the bag. Sofia. "How many?"

"Seventeen."

Pecan arrives but the whiskey on his breath arrived seconds earlier. He invades Sofia's space. "What's your name, pretty lady?"

Sofia points to her name on the bag.

He says, "Sofia. I like the way that sounds." He leans in close enough to lick her eye lashes. "You ain't gotta be scared of me."

Into the kitchen steps the youngest of the three women. According to the bag in her hand, she goes by Mila. Dark circles under her eyes. Sweat streams down her forehead.

She was pale before, but now she's ghostly. She saves Sofia from Pecan but doesn't seem to realize or care.

Pecan grabs the bag from her. "How many?"

Her voice cracks. Only one word and even that is too much for her to say with any conviction. "Fifteen." The apparition shuffles to the couch and lays down.

I state the obvious. "There's something wrong with her."

Pecan turns to me. "What of it?"

Sofia uses the moment to break from Pecan and rush back to the bathroom.

He watches her ass until it vanishes into the bathroom, then turns to me with a grin. "Time to get right." Two violet pills appear and find their way onto the kitchen counter where they get crushed with the back of a spoon, then lined. He rolls a five-dollar bill and hands it to me.

If I say no, he'll think it suspicious. Even if my refusal has nothing to do with being a cop. Promises were made. Sorry, Naomi. If the plan is for me to return safely, this is a necessary evil. I take the rolled five and snort the line.

The bill gets passed back to Pecan. He glances around the kitchen, and when he sees that Ve is still on the front porch with her guns, he whispers, "You looking to score some extra cash?"

Every word these people utter feels like entrapment. "With Broadway?"

"This ain't got nothin' to do with Ve or Broadway."

Ve's joint was an act of mercy. An attempt to even out the new guy. And here's Pecan, crushing up violet and helping me climb once again. They've reduced me to a patch of dirt in need of conquering. A beach worthy of storming.

I am Bull Run. I am Verdun. I am Normandy.

Fidget Electric tells me to question everything. Then it chastises me for being paranoid.

The violet line disappears up his nostril. "You interested or not?"

"Let's hear it."

He squeezes his nostrils closed for a moment. He knows what I know.

The drip is the best part. It's when the abyss first tickles your feet.

Eyes closed, Pecan says, "I got this, friend. Hit a jewelry store somewhere south of here. He's coming to town to fence it."

"Where's he coming from?"

Pecan opens his eyes. Studies me. "Doesn't matter. When he gets here, I'm gonna set him up with a guy I know handles this sorta thing. I need you to come with. Hang out. Look tough. If shit goes sideways, I need someone who can handle themselves."

I ask, "Pay?"

He glances over his shoulder to make sure Ve's still outside. "Three grand for a day's work. But you can't tell Ve or anybody else."

"Let me think on it."

"Damn, New Guy. Either you're in or out. Right here, right now."

At the diner he was making veiled threats. Now he needs my help on a side job Ve doesn't know about. If this is a test, I pass by taking the job. "I'm in."

— · —

Ten

Pecan pulled rank and told me to check on the cargo.

I'm in this cramped bathroom leaning against the door. The room writhes. Tile sweats. Grout crawls with gray veins. A room the same color as a sick tooth. The smell is language. Brown syllables. Acid grammar. Mint trying to make peace with rot.

The toilet crouches in the corner like a guilty thought. Lotte sits on it. Her face strained. Every few seconds there's a *plop, plop, plop,* and the stress leaves her for a few moments before it returns again.

Plop, plop, plop.

The sink gurgles small secrets. Sofia uses toothpaste to clean the pellets. The mirror sags; it wants to melt off the wall. The pipes underneath mumble in stomach tones.

Air clings to me. Thick. Sweet. Wrong. Scents overlap to form new sensations. Something animal. Something chemical. An apology meant to be decoded at a later date.

To anyone who wants to answer, I ask, "Where are you all from?"

Sofia doesn't even look up from her work with the toothpaste. "Belarus."

I ask, "Who do you work for?"

Through clenched teeth, Lotte says, "Same as you."

The light above flickers in long blinks. The floor swells like skin. The ceiling dips closer. Curious to see how this will end. Every sound turns liquid only to drip back into itself.

Mila's in the dry bathtub. Fully dressed and holding her stomach. Somehow, she's managed to look worse. My gut tells me what my mind doesn't want to hear.

When this is over, Mila won't have sixty pellets.

The smell follows the thought. The toothpaste tries to fight it, loses again. The room keeps breathing, slow, wet, endless.

A sound comes slow. Pressed through water and metal before it hits me. Air hiccupping. A cough made of glass. Walls quiver in sympathy. Tiles rattle. Grout crawls faster with veins pulsing violet.

It arrives in layers. First is heat. Curling along my spine and settling in my elbows. Second layer is a tremor I can feel under the soles of my feet. Third layer is color. Orange flashes in the air and bloom into green and silver and vanish before they register.

Pipes gurgle. Tiles sigh. The mirror flickers, warps, and my reflection licks the sound in a slow, crooked grin. The echo trails down the hallway. Ricocheting off every edge of the room, dragging the smell of metal and wet pine with it.

Another shot. A ghost of itself bending sideways, not the same as the first but carrying its pulse. I can taste it in the toothpaste ghost. Feel it pooling in the grout veins.

I'm not sure who fired or why, only that the sound has found a place to live inside me, curling its small, violent tongue around my pulse.

The forest has barked and it requires an answer. An investigation. My hand is already on the doorknob and then I'm in the kitchen and then Pecan has his gun out and is headed to the door and I don't know what else to do, so I follow him onto the porch.

The bag of guns is there, but Ve's gone. Pecan has his gun up and ready. The air is still. A warning to the two confused men on the porch. I pull my gun and wait. For what, who knows. Muscles stiffen. I try to tame my cop instincts.

Pecan calls out. "Ve!"

If there's a god, hopefully he commanded the forest to swallow her whole. With any luck, he'll do the same to me and Pecan so the women can go free.

But I have to get back to Naomi.

Promises were made.

A bird of prey circles above the treeline. Something is dead. Hopefully it's Ve. If she's gone, I can shoot Pecan and escape with the ladies from Belarus. If Reid has any reservations, I'll tell him I had to save the women.

Then I'll spend the rest of my life as a father and husband on the run with his family.

Scenarios fragment and reconfigure. Pecan scans the area with his back to me. Regardless of Ve's current status, I could put a bullet in his brain right here, right now. Have his body hit the ground and watch his memories leak out of his head. With him gone, it would only be a matter of killing Ve.

If she's not already dead.

My body turns towards him. Ready to change the dynamic. My finger strokes the trigger in anticipation. The forest watches me. Their betrayal means my death. My teeth grind, but this has to be done. This is the moment. Save the women. Save myself.

"Who the hell is that?" Pecan's voice is a brick through the window, shattering my concentration.

Emerging from the forest is Ve and some guy. As they draw closer, my mistake becomes evident. The person with Ve isn't some guy. It's a kid. Maybe a high schooler. Terrified and swamped in camo he has yet to grow into. In one hand, Ve has her handgun. Hunting rifle slung across her back. Her pace is furious, and the teenager struggles to keep up.

They arrive on the porch. Ve heads straight for the door without a glance in our direction. "This is Jimmy. He's going to be joining us."

As Jimmy passes, blood and brain matter reveal themselves in his hair, neck, and the left side of his face.

ELEVEN

TAXIDERMIED EYES WATCH THE congregation. Bodiless gods studying a chessboard.

Pecan forces a massage upon Sofia's shoulders.

Mila sits on the edge of the couch. Her hands clutch her stomach, desperate to contain whatever wants to break free. Lotte rubs her back.

In the middle of the room, Ve circles the kid. "Everyone, this is Jimmy. He's going to be joining us for a bit. His grandpa is no longer with us." She stops and marvels at the side of the kid's face. Crimson with bits of cottage cheese texture. "Well, maybe some of him is." Amused, she shifts her focus to me and reveals perfect teeth when the corners of her mouth rise.

I want to widen her smile with a butter knife.

She killed this kid's grandpa to try and flush out the truth of who I am.

Ve shifts her gaze from my eyes to my hands. They're twitching and she clocks it. She sucks her teeth and says, "You alright, New Guy?"

"I'm fine."

Ve reaches into her pocket. Pulls out a violet pill. Tosses it to me like she's feeding her favorite mammal at the aquarium. I catch it in my mouth. Clap my hands seal-style.

Mila stands. Opens her arms. Tilts her head to the ceiling and shrieks, "I am the new god!" Ragged air wheezes from her lungs as her body heaves with every breath. Lotte retreats into the couch and everyone turns to the possessed woman with the raccoon eyes. "I am the new god." She sprints to the wall behind Ve, places her palms against it, and slams her forehead into the wall. "I am the new god!" Slams her head into the wall a second time. Blood from her forehead fills the crater left by her forehead.

Pecan says, "The fuck is wrong with her?"

Mila pants. "I shall be free!" She slams her head into the wall again. The gash on her forehead opens wider, exposing the viscera underneath. Blood covers her face and the room stinks of copper and sweat. "I shall be free!" She pulls her head further back for more force.

Crack. She stumbles back. Exposing the dent in her head. Her legs go wobbly. The congregation observes in stunned silence.

Ve steps towards Mila. "Look at me."

Concussed and barely able to stand, Mila glares at Ve. "I am the new god. I must be released."

Ve says, "I can help you with that." She raises her gun and points it directly at Mila's face. "Are you ready to be free?"

"Yes."

A burst. Like a heartbeat inside a skull. The room shudders. Chemical solvents smell like perfume. Mila's body goes limp and hits the floor. The hole in her head bubbles. Blood from her face retreats back into the hole. Mila's lifeless face bubbles with distorted anguish. Elongating and contorting.

Something is trying to get out of her head.

Out of the hole emerges a fuchsia otherness. An unending steam shrouds the room in a cumulus textured pink. There's no end in sight as the haze thickens and suffocates. It stings my eyes and nostrils. Battery acid with the sweetness of licorice. The only thing visible is the new god in all its pink splendor. A mist hovering like sewer steam in the early morning.

And in a moment, it dissipates. Sucked into the gaping mouths and between the clenched teeth of the fur covered gods perched on the walls. Elk. Wolf. Bear. Each doing their part to save us from this formless evil. What doesn't get sucked into their mouths, escapes into the walls, the ceiling, and the floorboards. The room is clear of the fuchsia, but my gut tells me this will not be the last we see of it.

Ve holds a hunting knife out to me, handle first. "I still need to get my drugs out of her." For a moment I stare at the knife in her hand. And then I realize what she wants me to do. I take the handle and wait for further instructions. Instead, she says, "Everyone back to what you were doing."

Lotte and Sofia shuffle back into the bathroom.

I kneel next to the body. I haven't dissected anything since high school. My body trembles at the thought of what they want me to do. Mila is so full of pellets, she didn't soil herself when she died. It's the closest thing there is to a silver lining.

Pecan says, "You should take her clothes off."

Ve says, "And don't cut too deep. There's still some inventory in there." Then she takes a seat on the couch and pats the space next to her. "Come sit with me Jimmy." The kid does as he's instructed. Ve puts her arm around him and asks, "How old are you, Jimmy?"

Between whimpers, Jimmy answers, "Twelve."

Ve says, "Tell me, Max, what should we do with twelve-year-old Jimmy?"

"I wouldn't have brought him here in the first place." I fumble with the bottom of the hooded sweatshirt. Getting it up over her breasts is a bit of a struggle, but not as much of a struggle as getting it over her bloody head.

Ve says, "Let's not focus on the problem. Let's focus on the solution."

We both know she doesn't care about solutions. She brought him here to gauge my response. See if protector instincts get the better of me. "What do you want me to say? Kill him?"

She says, "Is that what you think we should do? Kill him?" She points her gun at the kid.

Swear to God I'll shoot her before I kill this kid. They'll have to kill me. Hurting a twelve-year-old is where I draw the line. Reid, the crew, my cover, all of it be damned. "That's not my answer."

The elk's eyes are clouded in pink.

The only sound is the kid sniffling. He's fighting the urge to cry, but his heart and tear ducts are winning out.

The grey sweatshirt is finally off, revealing a purple bra underneath. It has to be a coincidence. Purple is a popular color. This has nothing to do with the crushed and un-crushed pills overriding my system.

"Then what is your answer?" Ve's voice is listless. As if she's got somewhere better to be and all this is an inconvenience. Bold, considering it's a situation of her making.

I roll the body to the side to access the bra from the back. "He stays here with us. Alive. If someone heard your gun, we may need a bargaining chip."

Ve lowers her gun, and my heart no longer wants to be freed of my chest. "Hear that, Jimmy? You've been promoted from hostage to bargaining chip." She stands and turns to Pecan. "Find something to tie our friend up with."

My fingers find the clasp and work the bra off. Blood hasn't stopped leaking from her head and it's all over my hands, forearms, and jeans.

"And Jimmy," Ve continues, "before this is over, I'm going to ask you to tell me a joke. If I laugh, you go free. Guess what happens if I don't laugh?"

"You'll... kill me?"

Ve musses his hair the way you would if you were reminding your younger brother who the eldest is. "Very good. And Jimmy, no knock-knock jokes. You're better than that."

She makes her way to the kitchen, and I'm left trying to undress a corpse so I can cut it open and fish out balloons filled with violet pills. My fingers slip inside the elastic waist of the skirt, and it dawns on me that the best way to do this is to pull the panties down with the skirt. I adjust the fingers so they're under the panties and pull both the panties and the skirt down at the same time and slide them over her feet painted with blue nail polish.

And now I'm staring at a nude corpse so fresh it's still bleeding from the bullet hole.

Wolf god froths at the mouth. Pink bubbles cover the corners where lips meet cheeks. The gods are disappointed in me. But if they're truly gods, they know there's no other choice. Retrieve the drugs or die. I bring the knife over her stomach. Plunging the tip too deep could cut open the containers inside. The worst thing is breaking open another container and having to fish individual pills out of her stomach.

This requires a surgeon's precision.

Best to start on her chest, between her breasts. This way, the knife can slide down. Get a running start, so to speak. Then I can filet her open at the stomach and hopefully get in, snag the cargo, and get out as quickly as possible.

There's a slight give and then the tip hits her breastplate. It should be deep enough to open her, but not so deep it'll cut open the treasure inside.

Treasure? Fuck. This cabin. These people. This job. Who I was has slipped into the tide. Tumbling and fighting the current. Air. Water. Sky. Air, Water. Sky. The lies fill my lungs and threaten to end me before Ve or Pecan have a chance.

On autopilot, the knife slides from her chest to her stomach. One vertical line gets crossed by three horizontal lines. I dig my fingers into the opening and pull the skin and muscle apart. There's resistance. But the body opens before me like a red cathedral. The light pools inside the cavity, glinting off the wet sheen of organs that ten minutes ago rose and fell in slow rhythm, each one alive in its own quiet motion. The air is heavy with death and sweat.

Death is from her. Sweat is from my nerves.

My body heaves. It's too much. Bile assaults my taste buds, but every chunk gets sent back down.

Inside is red and white and shadow. My hand hovers, trembling just above the edge of the chasm, as if the body itself has swallowed what's mine. This is not just flesh. It was someone's daughter. A sister. A loved one. Someone may have depended on her. Maybe that's how she got here. Trying to do right by someone she loved.

A son. A daughter. Both.

The liver glistens, almost black in the light. Veins stand like blue roots. Somewhere in this labyrinth, little balloons are hidden, claimed by the dark warmth of the body.

I reach in. The heat grips my hand instantly, enveloping the wrist and the forearm. It feels alive. The body knows and so it holds me, refusing to give back what I've been ordered to retrieve.

She's not here but she's everywhere. My hands won't listen. They swim. Everything's breathing, too close, too full. Something inside her jiggles when I touch it. Or maybe it's me. Maybe it's the room trying to remember a time before we barged in ushering death and new gods.

There's color under my nails. Dark but red. The tips of my fingers slide past once vital organs. My hands and arms have been plunged into a pot of spaghetti and marinara sauce. I keep looking for the things that were supposed to matter. But I'm not sure any of this matters anymore. There's no good in this place. Only tiers of awfulness. Some lower than others, but none are worthy of pride.

I whisper sorry, or maybe I don't. The walls lean in. The world blinks slow. I'm slipping sideways, soft and hollow, holding nothing but mush and intestines in need of cutting.

My hand comes out and the cavity gurgles. My other hand, the one still inside, pulls up a bulging tube, and the free hand uses the knife to cut it open. Both hands work in unison to squeeze out what's inside.

Out drops something foreign. Into the muck of a decaying body. My hands go in. Searching for something that shouldn't be in the human body. It's not just the feel. It's the movement. My hands turn over, searching for more. My fingers touch a couple other objects.

This has to be them.

I call out, "How many should still be in her?"

Ve says, "There should be nineteen left. But let's assume some of them burst and introduced her to the new god."

The cabin has shrunk since I started this hunt. Air is made of wet paper and regret. I try to stay upright, but the floor tilts like it's trying to tip me into her absence. Outside, the forest hums the same low song over and over. It might be wind. It might be the end of something. I can't tell which.

First two pellets are extracted. Now it's back into the soup for the other seventeen.

Twelve

Nearly all the soap is gone but my hands and arms are still stained from Mila's poisoned blood.

Her poison is my poison. Motivation is what sets us apart.

Sofia cleans Mila's seventeen pellets in the bathroom.

The body continues to stain the floor in the main section of the cabin.

Pecan puts the finishing touches on the rope, confining Jimmy to the chair at the kitchen table.

Ve is out front. Doing whatever the hell Ve does.

I have failed Mila. All I can do now is save Sofia, Lotte, and the kid. Bonus points if I can do it without getting myself killed.

Pecan pats the top of the kid's head. "Don't go anywhere, you little shit." He arrives next to me. Pleased with himself and full of moxie. "They should be rid of those pellets soon. You should take the older one. She'd be good for you. Bet she bucks like a bronco."

I walk to the opposite end of the kitchen, away from the kid, and motion for Pecan to follow me. When he's close enough, I whisper, "Do all of Ve's jobs turn into shit shows?"

"Most, not all." Pecan studies the sobbing kid at the table.

"And what's the deal with her bringing that kid in and exposing us all like that?"

Pecan says, "I'm sure she has her reasons."

"I say we talk to Ve. Get a meeting with Broadway."

Pecan scoffs at the idea. "And do what? Air our grievances? I hate to break it to you, New Guy, but there's no HR department."

"Look, I know you got your eyes open for other opportunities. All I'm saying, maybe we take some steps to try and get into middle management."

"Sounds like mutiny."

As the front door opens, I say, "Just a couple of guys talking business."

Halfway in the cabin, Ve says, "Max, I need you to dig a couple of graves. Make sure they're deep enough so the toes don't stick out."

Thirteen

In one hand, a shovel. In the other, Mila's ankle.

The carcass drags behind me, leaving a trail from the cabin to the front yard and deeper into the belly of this unnatural beast.

Ponderosa Pines rise like ribs. Wide and breathing. Their orange skin catches the last of the dying light and saturates into hues before morphing with the fluidity of a lava lamp. This new world creaks inward. Slow and endless. Turning itself over in sleep. A beast primordial. Beneath me, the ground moves in slow muscle shifts. Deep and secret. A living thing rearranging its bones.

The air hangs heavy. The inside of something vast. A creature older than sound, dreaming me into its lungs. The bark glows hypnotic. Veins of rust and gold sliding between the trunks. I drag the body over stumps and rocks, through dirt, leaving liquid breadcrumbs the color of death. A parasite crawling through organs the shape of something unknown, leaving a trail to find its way back out.

Every branch bends like thought. Watching. Reaching. Sap drips like breath. Night doesn't exist in this place that's swallowed me. Only grey sky and orange bones. Still, the corpse and I press forward. Somewhere above, a crow splits the silence, but it doesn't echo. It disappears, absorbed.

The beast smells of death and bile and something otherworldly. A sweetness processed through a crack in time. Jimmy's grandpa comes into view. Right where Ve said he would be. Mila and I arrive next to him. His cratered face is alive with early rot and flies. One of his eyes has gone missing. Dinner for a vulture or some other scavenger who calls this creature home.

One hole deep enough for both of the bodies I couldn't save will be the quickest way to handle the task. If I'm lucky enough to survive this, I'll come back with the authorities. We'll get these bodies to their families for a proper burial. Giving their loved ones a chance to mourn is the least I can do.

The shovel doesn't dig so much as argue with the ground. Each push sinks into something that was once harder, younger. The dirt clings in clumps that twitch, not wanting to be moved. Heavy in the way your arms would feel after swimming in buttermilk.

The handle pulses against my palms, alive and whispering in a language made of effort. Every thrust sends a shiver up my arms. Enveloping me in a warmth I've never known. The blade bites earth and surrenders to rock. Gashes roots. Every crunch echoes flat and disturbed.

Sweat escapes my skin as the hole expands sideways, stretching into silhouette. I keep going, half sure the dirt's laughing, half sure it's waiting for me to stop pretending I'm the one doing the digging.

My pace quickens and my muscles respond with acid. Pecan could be doing any number of things right now, including assaulting the remaining women. If this task takes too long, I could be back in the beast with another grave to dig.

Another body to retrieve at a later date.

Another family with a delayed ceremony.

The beast sighs. Windswept coldness chills my damp skin. The trees lean in. Listening. It passes through me before my body can recognize its touch. It carries a whisper. Something older trying to remember how to speak. Low and barely audible.

You know why you took this assignment.

A question from a place that's tapped into my mind and heart. Pushing forward guilt and fear and making me question my own motives.

Another sigh carries more whispers that I try to ignore.

A real man would be with his pregnant wife.

The goal has always been to make this world a better place, starting with my city. Cleanse it of the filth and crime and drugs and corruption. Free it from mutilation and greed.

All the things that I've become. All the things I'm now a party to.

Jimmy's grandpa turns to me and the two holes in his face merge to form a smile unlike any other. Happy and demonic. Terrifying and comforting. His lips never move. The smile never wavers. His voice is gruff and low, and it settles on me from somewhere deep within the creature.

Only a coward uses work to hide from responsibility.

It comes thin and sideways. From above and below. The sound of memories cracking open. A laugh so soft it can't belong to grandpa. A cackle so harsh it can't be from Mila. It skips between the pines. Rolls against liquid bark and touches everything once.

And then it's gone and only the wind remains.

But the wind doesn't know jokes so cruel.

Fourteen

The bodies are in the ground, and I pray they don't claw their way out.

The cabin sits where it always has, but now it's grown bones. The walls glitter under the dying light. Skin turned to violet crystal. Ribs of quartz push through the wood, like something decided halfway to stop pretending it was a cabin. The porch droops under its new weight. Jaws sag open with translucent boards and pulse faintly with trapped air bubbles the shape of frozen screams.

The windows have sealed over with a milky film. Calcified membranes hold the last breath of whatever it was meant to be. The roof slouches heavy with mineral bloom. Stalactites of sap and salt drool from the eaves. Every nail glows like the embers of an angry fire.

Less built. More grown. Time forgot the difference between wood and bone, memory and mineral. The forest leans in to watch the cabin breathe. Slow and content, dreaming in stone.

The entrance is covered with shards of crystal bone that radiate when touched by breath. The only way in is through the shards. And the only way through is with this shovel. Tired but determined, my muscles work to bring the shovel up high over my head and then crashing down into the barrier. Over and over again. The sparks illuminate the grey in a brilliant flash of warmth and orange and red and electricity. For an instant, everything is bright and blinding and beautiful in its radiance.

Pecan appears. Out of the crystal. Staring at me with exhausted eyes. "The fuck you doing, New Guy?"

An answer doesn't formulate. Instead, I step inside.

Lotte and Sofia are on their knees, cleaning up the mess from my dissection. They dip white rags stained pink into a pot of pink water and use it to smear pink slurry all over the floor. In another universe they may be cleaning it. But here and now, they're only making it worse.

Some stains are destined to linger.

Jimmy no longer cries. Now he sits with a blank expression. A twelve-year-old aged a hundred years in under three hours.

Ve sits at the table across from him. She pulls out an envelope. "Ladies, would you be so kind to join us for a moment?"

Happy for the reprieve, Sofia and Lotte toss their rags into the bucket and head to the kitchen where they flank Jimmy.

The envelope in Ve's hand has Mila's name scribbled on it. She opens it and pulls out a stack of cash. "You got a mom and dad, Jimmy?"

"Yes."

Ve uses the cash to point and emphasize the words as she speaks. "What do they do for work?"

"Mom teaches fourth grade. Dad works in construction."

Ve points the money at Sofia and then Lotte. "Now, ladies, I know this has been a little traumatic for you. After all, you signed on to be mules for Broadway. You didn't fly across the world with bellies full of dope only to land in America and clean blood off the floor. Did you?"

Both women nod in agreement.

"But things happen." Ve uses her thumb to flip through the bills. "And since Mila isn't around to collect her payment, I thought, hey, why not split this money between you three? Now, Jimmy, do you know what hush money is?"

The kid's breath catches in his throat. His voice croaks out the first word. "Money you pay me to be quiet."

"Very good, Jimmy." Ve's eyes go wide with the sparkle of a proud teacher. "You only get this money if your joke makes me laugh. But if you leave with my money, and then I hear about you ratting me out, I'm going to go to your mom's class and kill everyone in there, starting with those fourth graders. Then I'll go to your daddy's construction site and kill all the people he works with. Do you believe I'll do it?"

Jimmy nods his head *yes*.

Ve starts to separate the money into three different piles.

Pecan waltzes into the kitchen and chugs half the remaining bottle of whiskey and then wipes his mouth with his forearm. "Hey, Ve. New Guy wants to meet Broadway."

Ve continues to divvy up the money. "All I wanted was to come here, relax, collect my drugs, and clean my guns. Is that so much to ask?"

Pecan says, "New Guy wants to climb the corporate ladder. He considers you middle management."

He wants me dead, and if I don't say something he's gonna get his wish. "Seems strange. Working for someone I've never met."

Ve says, "Tell yourself you work for me. Problem solved." She hands a stack of cash to Lotte, then another to Sofia. She holds up the final stack and points it at Sofia.

"Put this in Jimmy's pocket." Sofia takes the money. Ve turns to me and says, "Is that what I am to you? Middle management?"

The words tumble out of my mouth. I'm not sure if it's instinct or Fidget Electric. "I just want to make sure I keep getting work with you guys, and face time with the big guy could help with that."

Ve delivers a pouty face worthy of a Golden Globe. "Are the bills piling up, Max?"

"Pecan offered me a job, so I took it. But I'd rather work exclusively with you and Broadway."

Ve's mood shifts from playful to deadly and she aims it right at Pecan. "You offered Max a job?"

He stammers. "Uhhh, I, Uhh... I got a friend coming to town and I was looking to score some extra scratch. Figured I could bring Max along."

I say, "No disrespect, Ve. I'm just looking for a chance to move up with you guys."

Ve lays her head on the table. "Is this the part of the interview where you tell me you want my job in five years?"

The knot in my stomach pulls inward. "You don't seem to be on board. Let's forget the whole thing."

Ve stands. "Of course I'm on board. As middle management—"

"I never said you were middle management."

Pecan slams his fist on the kitchen counter. "Yes, you did."

Ve's voice climbs a few octaves. "Enough!" The cabin falls silent. She lets the air sit. Heavy and tense. Her eyes glance from me to Pecan to Lotte to Sofia and finally on the kid. "What would you do, Jimmy?"

Jimmy clears his throat. "My dad always says happy employees make for a successful company."

Ve positions herself behind the kid and massages his scalp. "Meeting Broadway would require a promotion. And the organization only has enough space for one person to advance." She leans in and whispers in his ear more seductively than any woman should whisper to a child. "What happens to the one who doesn't get promoted? Can't keep him around. He'll be jealous. And jealousy leads to all sorts of drama. I hate drama."

The kid thinks for a moment. "Well, maybe when you give the promotion to one of them, their first job could be to kill the one who didn't get promoted."

Ve kisses him on the forehead. "I like where your head's at, kid."

Fifteen

Grind my skull into sand and snort it until there's nothing left.

Pay no mind to Lotte on the toilet. Straining to push out plastic pellets full of violet-colored pills.

Pay no mind to the oppressive bitterness assaulting my nostrils.

Pay no mind to the mirror and the melting reflection.

One pill on the counter. Credit card on the pill. Palm on the credit card.

Push.

"Maybe you shouldn't take more, no?"

The voice belongs to Sofia. How long has she been here?

How long has she been watching me?

How long have I cared?

My response is a hiss. Long and angry. A serpent protecting its eggs.

Crush it.

Crunch. Pill becomes powder.

Promises were made.

Line it.

Sorry, Naomi. I need strength to save the world.

Snort it.

It hits like a rambling wreck marauding the hillside. Screaming and carrying siege weapons.

I can taste the brown bitterness in the air.

Humidity wraps its arms around me and squeezes.

It's all electric and it feels like home.

Gliding through the cabin like the hologram of a dead celebrity.

My skull screams but my mouth stays shut.

Something pounds on the walls. They bulge and brace for impact. Whatever wants in is desperate and won't be stopped by drywall.

From his spot on the wall, the elk watches us. Tonguing the pink film covering its teeth.

The wolf growls. Low and aggressive until its face contorts from anguish or disappointment.

The bear stays silent, allowing its face to expand and contract with boils primed to burst. When they do, pink steam goes free and finds a home in the ceiling.

Pressure builds behind my eyes, and I hope when my eyes pop out of my head, one of them will land in Pecan's mouth and the other will find a home in Ve's throat.

With any luck they'll both choke.

Then I could take Lotte and Sofia and the kid and get the hell out of here. Free them and be the hero the city needs.

Or simply let them go and stay behind to deal with the demon god trying to infiltrate our world.

Ve and Pecan and their crew and their purple pills from Belarus are the least of my worries.

We've released something dangerous. Something that could spell the end for all humanity.

The end for Naomi and the child inside of her.

I must save the world.

And if I can bring down this crew in the process, all the better.

Elk. Wolf. Bear. All laughing.

The pounding intensifies. Could be in my head. Could be in the walls.

Nobody else seems to hear it. They're busy watching me watch them.

Ve seems amused. She has no idea the new god is arriving.

Pecan seems tired. Too weary to help me in the fight for our reality. It's okay. He can't be trusted anyway. He thinks I killed his brother. Maybe a previous version of me did. It's so hard to keep track of these things.

The lies I've told them.

The lies I've told myself.

The lies I've told Naomi.

Pecan's lips are moving but the words are muffled. Gurgles from a drowning man. I squint my eyes to hear him better, and now I'm questioning why I thought that would even work.

Wait. Am I breathing?

A gasp. Musty air fills my lungs.

Pecan says, "Hey, New Guy. Your face is leaking."

My fingers move to investigate, and sure enough, my brain is escaping through my nose.

The new god has chosen the field of battle.

Sixteen

Sofia hands a bag full of pellets to Pecan, and he licks his lips.

Cracks reach for the ceiling. Plaster and paint won't restrain it for long.

Pecan says, "So you're all emptied out?" He sets the bag of pellets on the kitchen counter. "I'm thinking you and I head into the bedroom. Dirty the sheets."

Pounding from below shakes the floor. Pink mist dampens the countertops like morning dew.

Sofia says, "I have a boyfriend."

Pecan sucks his teeth. "We don't have to tell him."

My nostrils are caked with blood. It itches and cracks, then itches some more. Only a matter of time before my upper lip is covered in blood and mucus.

Pecan says, "I'm just trying to be friendly."

Part of me is waiting for Ve to intervene so I don't have to blow my cover. Female solidarity coming to all our rescue. But she pays no attention to what's happening in the kitchen.

Sofia says, "No thank you."

I say, "We need to count those pellets. Make sure she delivered all of them."

Pecan grabs her hand. "Go for it." He puts his other hand on top of hers. Shaking deli meat between two slices of ill intent.

"We got a job to do." My voice comes out a little higher than warranted, but I need to be heard over the cracking of the foundation.

Finally, Pecan acknowledges me. "Enough with the cock blocking."

"Give it a rest." Muscles tense. Ready for a fight. Guns or fists. Whatever he wants. "She's not interested."

Pecan drops her hand and it's a small victory. "Doesn't matter if she's interested." Sofia tries to run away, but Pecan grabs her by the arm. His other hand pulls out his gun and points it at my face. "Why'd you take my brother through the back of the house? Away from the rest of us?"

Now we see what's really going on. Wolf and bear howl with delight. Two beasts starved for entertainment.

This isn't about me or Sofia. It's about him. Lifelong tough guy trying to figure out how to grieve for his dead brother.

Pecan says, "My brother would have gone out shooting. I know him. He was a badass sonofabitch. But you lead him out the back where none of us could see what you had planned."

"The van was on fire. Cops were everywhere." My stomach twists. Hot magma rises inside me.

Pecan takes a step towards me, and my hand moves to my gun. "Strip."

Ve slinks into the kitchen with a freshly cleaned assault rifle in her hand.

"I'm not taking my clothes off for you." I lean back against the counter and face forward so Ve is in the corner of my left eye, while Pecan is in the corner of my right. Above me is the cracking ceiling. Below me is the bulging floor.

Sofia makes it into the living room and gets to the other side of the couch.

The kid's eyes sprint across the cabin. Pecan. Ve. Sofia. Me. Back to Pecan. Rinse. Repeat.

Pecan says, "We need to see if you're wearing a wire, officer."

I say, "You call me a cop again and you better chase it with a bullet."

Pecan's finger massages the trigger. "Don't threaten me with a good time, asshole."

Ve raises her assault rifle. "I'm gonna need you to take off your clothes, Max. Nice and slow, like you're working for tips."

The elk hums. Low and patient. Sound folding air into slow waves. Each note rises through the floor and into my legs, until I'm certain the boards are breathing beneath me.

The bear watches. Its glassy eyes clouded pink. From its muzzle drifts a thin sweetness, honey-dust and smoke, the scent of something that used to be alive and still hasn't decided otherwise.

I slide off my t-shirt with the pit stains and toss it to the floor.

The stove ticks. Metal lips loosen, releasing murmurs I can't make out, but the tone is a prayer. Confessions through rusted appliances.

I kick off my shoes and undo my pants.

Dust rises from the floor in slow ribbons, plunging the room into paleness. It gathers on my bare shoulders until I'm part of the display. Another creature pinned to the quiet.

I slide my pants down and hope my underwear is still clean.

Somewhere under the floors, inside the walls, in the ceiling, the hum deepens, stretching toward a rhythm too

large for this place. A mouth of old wood and bone, waiting for the perfect time to engulf us.

I stand in the room on full display in nothing but socks
and boxer-briefs.

Ve says, "Lower the damn gun, Pecan."

"It doesn't mean he ain't a cop."

Ve aims her gun at Pecan and he reluctantly takes the
hint. His gun lowers and it's a perfect time to get dressed.

If I ever see Reid again, I'm gonna punch him in his
fucking face.

Seventeen

They approach you with promises of plaques and medals and ceremonies where everyone smiles and says you're a hero and tells you how you should run for office.

They promise you promotions and raises and higher rungs on the org chart.

You think it sounds great. Prestigious. You think it'll prove you're brave and honorable.

You think it proves you're a real man. Or it proves you're every bit as worthy as the fellas.

You think it'll make your parents proud and your community safe.

You do it for the pension.

You do it for your family.

You do it for your kid who hasn't crawled out the womb yet.

But somehow in doing it, you betray the ones you're trying to impress. The ones you're trying to save.

You miss birthdays.

You miss date nights.

You miss ultrasounds.

And then, before you know it, you've sacrificed every-thing, and the war rages on with no end in sight.

You're a hollowed husk of memories you never made and laughter you heard about secondhand.

And somewhere in there you wonder if you joined this war because you didn't actually want to be there for those things anyway.

Those obligations don't feed you. Don't nourish your hunger for greatness.

If you had been there to be the plus one at the office party, for the cookout, for the show, or for whatever was on the calendar on whatever day, you'd be normal.

And you're anything but normal.

It's the reason you joined the force in the first place. You were destined for extraordinary things.

And what did your pursuit of deliver you?

Instead of listening to a little one kick inside a belly, you're preparing to be the front line of defense in a battle against something unspeakable.

Instead of putting a crib together, you're in this cabin with the guy whose brother you killed, and in order to stay alive, you have to prove you're not the person you actually are.

Self-reflection is no longer a priority. There's a god in the walls in need of a sacrifice.

And then the crazy woman with the assault rifle takes a seat across from the kid, props her gun against the table, and says, "Boy, that was tense." She leans forward and locks in on the terrified twelve-year-old. "Got any good jokes, Jimmy?"

Light no longer illuminates. It creeps. Along the walls. Across the floor. Arthritic fingers stretching across the ceiling. Crystallizing into yellow shards and mocking gravity as it drips upwards and sideways.

I'm fully dressed and keeping an eye on Pecan. My victory meant his defeat, and it's clear he's a sore loser.

Jimmy clears his throat.

Ve sits back and crosses her arms. She's in the front row at the comedy club and she's using her body to heckle the first-time comedian.

Jimmy clears his throat again. "There was this guy." A deep breath fails to round up some composure. "He just got out of prison, and he's only got like ten dollars. But he really wants to have sex, so the first thing he does is he goes to a place where they have hookers—"

Ve interjects. "Whorehouse."

Jimmy says, "Yeah. And so he goes. And when he gets in, the lady who owns it—"

Ve exhales. "Madam."

Jimmy continues. "Sorry. The madam lady tells him yeah, they got someone who will have sex with him for ten dollars. She says all he has to do is go upstairs and go into the last room on the left. She tells him to leave the lights off. She's already in bed waiting for him."

It's impossible to tell if Ve's amused by where this is headed, or counting the seconds until she can kill this kid.

The kid continues. "All he has to do is take off his clothes and climb on top of her. The guy is really excited. He runs up the stairs and goes into the room. He leaves the lights off and takes off his clothes."

When this goes south, there's no way for me to kill Ve and live. The second I draw on Ve, Pecan will gun me down. My only play is to make sure Pecan doesn't get me with a kill shot. Then I can have enough time to kill him. With the three of us gone, the kid and the two women can go free.

Ve leans forward, immersed in the joke.

The twelve-year-old notices and his confidence grows. "The guy climbs on top of her and starts having sex. But it's weird because she's totally quiet. After a while, he feels this weird stuff coming out of her mouth. He thinks it's spit, so he keeps going. Then it starts coming out of her nose. He gets off of her, puts his pants back on and runs back down to the madam lady. He says he doesn't know what happened, but he thinks that girl is sick. Her nose was running and she was drooling a lot. The madam lady opens the door to a back room and yells, 'Harold, the dead one's full again!'"

My hand hovers over my gun. I can feel Pecan's eyes on me, but I don't care. Air and electricity raise goose pimples on my skin. Eyes blink rapidly. All I want is a sign from Ve. *Let's all die in a hail of bullets.*

Or is she going to let this kid go?

Cracks stretch across the ceiling. Some type of otherness wants in through the ceiling.

Ve sits back in her chair and eyes Jimmy.

Curtains sway in perfect unison.

Ve grins. Then stifles a chuckle. But it won't be contained. It grows into a full-fledged laugh.

The kid beams.

Ve laughs so hard she snorts.

My hand eases away from the gun. I can't tell if Ve is loving the joke, or the fact a twelve-year-old told it.

Between snorts and gasps for air, Ve says, "New Guy. Untie the kid. He's free to leave."

EIGHTEEN

YELLOW WASHES THE CABIN from an unseen source.

A silhouette in the shape of Jimmy moves towards the door.

Ve's voice has too much timber in it. "Hey, kid." She waits until the shape of Jimmy turns to her, then continues. "Don't ever take shit from anyone. Got it?"

The shape of Jimmy nods its head and then proceeds to the front door.

Another figure, this one bigger, moves to block his exit. Pecan.

He stops in front of the door and raises his gun. Jimmy stands still.

So does time.

Pecan motions for Jimmy to take a step back and get next to Lotte.

Ve says, "What are you doing, Pecan?"

Pecan says, "I'm proving he's a cop." His gun shifts between the kid and Lotte. "Choose who dies, cop."

Lotte whimpers. "I still have your drugs in me."

Pecan aims his gun for her head. "We can get them after I gives your brains a way out."

Ve's voice marches out of her mouth. Assertive and pissed off. "I said the kid can go."

I take a step towards the kid, the mule, and the psychopath. "Point the gun at me, Pecan."

The gun shakes in his hand. He steadies it and points it at the kid's face. "Sounds like something a cop would say."

"Hey, asshole." Ve's voice echoes off the cracked walls. "I gave that kid my word. And if you shoot that mule. it's bad for business."

Tears stroll down Lotte's face like they have all the time in the world.

The kid straightens his back like he knows something we don't.

My hands go up. "Doing this doesn't prove anything."

Pecan points the gun at Lotte's face. "Admit you're a cop."

Jimmy swallows loud enough for everyone to hear it. He smirks at Pecan with the misplaced bravado only a child can muster. "How do we know you're not a cop?"

All the air seeps out through the cracks in the floor.

Who the hell is this kid?

Pecan points the gun at Lotte's face, then squeezes, and the clap echoes with distorted percussion.

For the second time today, Jimmy's face gets coated in someone else's blood.

Before Lotte's body can hit the floor, an automatic assault rifle purrs a violent melody, building and then collapsing into itself like a living thing choosing not to exist.

Pecan's chest tears open and his body spins, then stumbles backwards. His gun raises in Ve's general direction, then tumbles out of his hand. Another burst. Iron and powder taste like carbonated soda. What's left of Pecan stumbles back into the wall, then slumps to the floor, leaving a blood trail on the wall like an arrow pointing down.

Ve says, "I gave the kid my word. Without that, what am I?" Her voice carries a weight that doesn't suit the version of her I've been dealing with.

Outside the windows is the ocean and we're miles beneath the surface. Home to alien creatures who roam the depths for prey. A hammerhead drifts past like a thought that split itself in two and never healed, its body slicing the dusk in one long whisper of motion. The glass bends around it, pretending to be an ocean.

Behind it trails a jellyfish, soft and shining, a tangle of color that keeps forgetting what color it was. Its tendrils bloom and collapse in silence, a living lantern sinking upward. The two of them pass like a sentence full of misspelled words. Predator and prey gliding through the same dark grammar.

Jimmy says, "Thank you."

The window shivers once, holding the image too long, and I can't tell if I'm underwater or if the world outside is finally breathing like it always meant to.

Ve says, "You did good, kid." She finally lowers her gun and turns to Sofia. "Count Lotte's pellets. We need to know how many are still in her."

We've entered a cathedral made of breath and hunger. The world narrows to a tunnel of slick thunder, ribs creaking like ship timbers. Darkness prepares to swallow us whole.

Sofia scurries to the kitchen.

The air tastes of salt and storm. Salt thick on my tongue, the sour musk of old tides cling to the back of my throat. Every inhale is humid. My skin prickles with the unknown memory of ocean pressure, the water still clinging, whispering.

Ve says, "New Guy, you're gonna need to dig another hole."

My muscles go limp with the thought of it.

Silence is unfamiliar. The heart of the beast beats like a tide hammering a shore, slow and vast, shaking my bones until I can't tell where I end and its pulse begins. The sound of it drowns thought. Wet thunder. Guttural. Infinite. Somewhere, fluid drips, steady as a clock.

Ve continues to bark orders. "Hey, kid, you wanna earn a couple bucks?

The kid says, "Sure."

I can feel the slow undulation, muscles shifting like the walls of a sleeping giant. Flesh flexes. The world breathes. The cabin hums a low, mournful vibration that passes through teeth and down my spine. A prayer older than language.

Ve says, "I need you to cut open that body. Get the pellets out. Knife's in the bag."

Within living night, there is light, faint and strange: a greenish shimmer bleeding through translucent flesh, plankton ghosts swimming like constellations. It feels holy, in a way that makes my bones ache.

My gun is aimed at Ve. My voice is aimed at Jimmy. "Do not pick up that knife, kid."

Ve huffs. "The things you people make me do."

Somewhere between heartbeat and echo, a realization hits and everything falls into place. I say, "I can't let you ruin this kid, Broadway."

The floor sighs. The windowpanes shiver, their reflections rippling like disturbed water. Then the world forgets stillness.

Ve laughs. It feels too boisterous for the moment. "Did you hear his joke? The kid is already ruined. This is what we call the recruiting phase."

The cabin breathes. Walls flex inward and out, as if the forest itself has drawn a long, panicked breath. Every nail remembers it is separate from the wood. Beams groan like wounded animals. Dust drifts from the rafters in slow, golden cascades.

The fucking kid picks up the knife, and there's a strong chance he's going to move on me to prove his worth to Ve.

Brain waves crash against the shore. Thoughts pass in a blur. Did she hear me? Or does she think ignoring me will make the accusation go away? "You're not even going to deny it?"

Ve responds with a furrowed brow.

The ground lurches again. A deep, physical growl from the unseen bones of the earth. The furniture dances in a silent, drunken waltz. A lamp topples, light shattering into frantic shards.

I say, "There is no Broadway, is there?"

Ve leers at me. Her hand creeps towards her gun.

The kid has the knife in his hand.

Somewhere in the distance, a boulder splits like a cracked tooth, echoing through the valley.

My grip tightens on the gun. "Admit it. You're Broadway, aren't you?"

Ve asks, "What makes you say that?"

I grin and say, "You have no idea what I've had to do just to get these douche bags to respect me."

Ve's hand is almost poised to raise her assault rifle. "If you're gonna pull the trigger—"

The burst is loud enough to cave in the walls. Her face implodes and the hole sucks in all the air. The lack of air is suffocating for a moment, then things are back to normal.

Except for the three dead bodies emitting fuchsia smog into the cabin.

I wheel around and point my gun at Jimmy. It's not my intention to shoot him, but he's wielding a knife, and ever since he told that joke, he's acting more and more like Ve's protege.

There's a moment where he seems to wonder if he can win this fight. Me with my gun. Him with his knife. I say, "Put the knife down."

He shakes his head. "No."

And then, as suddenly as it began, everything fades into a silence swollen and uncertain. The cabin stands crooked and dazed. Its timbers tremble from the memory of motion. The forest holds its breath. Reality waits to see if it will keep itself together.

Sofia appears and covers Jimmy's hand with hers. Emotion pours from his eyes as she takes the knife out of his hand.

I say, "Go." My weapon gets holstered.

Sofia and Jimmy stagger to the door. When they reach it, Sofia sees through me. Her glare penetrates me to reveal my yesterday, today, and my tomorrow. "Are you police?"

"I am."

Jimmy's eyes are puffy from exhaustion and trauma. "You coming with us?"

Poor kid will be in therapy until his age hits triple digits.

"I can't. I gotta stay here and save the world."

Sofia asks, "From who?"

"From whatever's trying to get in." I wave them off for emphasis. They have to get out of here while they still can. "Now go. And tell Naomi I'm sorry. Not just about the drugs, but for everything."

Sofia asks, "Who's Naomi?"

I say, "A woman who deserves better."

Nineteen

Fidget Electric told me to get naked.

In the middle of the room. Nine-millimeter in one hand. Hunting knife in the other.

Pipes gurgle and moan. Pink steam spews from the bowels of the kitchen sink. All around me, the pink god pollutes the air.

It flows out of the fractures in the floor.

It seeps out of the electrical sockets.

It gushes from between the couch cushions.

It leaks from the hole in Lotte's head and from every bullet wound in Pecan's body and from the crater in Ve's face.

My body is full of violet. The cabin is full of pink.

Nostrils burn bright with a dull pain that warms my soul. This skin suit of mine is alive with a hundred thousand volts of angry electricity.

Ready to send the new god back to where it came from.

The first sound is a sucking rasp, like the world itself exhales through some impossible mouth. The cabin shudders. Walls twitch. At first, it's subtle. A tremor beneath the plaster. But soon, dark lines bulge and ripple across the wood. The cabin breathes from inside out.

A sticky tendril, slick with iridescent ooze, unfurls from a gaping hole where floor meets wall. It quivers. Tasting the air, then latches onto the table leg, pulling itself with a wet, sucking sound. I stumble backwards, my hands slide across a floor crawling with a latticework of writhing, translucent limbs. They coil around my bare legs. Clammy and clamorous, leaving a trail of cold slime that reeks of brine and rot.

My gun shatters the air. One bullet after another goes into the fray of tendrils and tentacles. Some bullets leave holes in the wall. But others penetrate my attackers. Puncture wounds fill and then leak viscous ooze the color of midnight. Thicker than oil, it stretches and drips, but it's not enough to stop their reaching.

Desperate to keep them at bay, my finger pulls the trigger until the gun is empty. Tentacles continue to reach from all around. The cabin wants me as a trophy. Rendered useless, I toss the gun at the nearest slime covered appendage. It catches the gun and tosses it aside.

The ceiling melts. Black and green veins pulse downward. Roots of a tree grown from a nightmare. Each tendril is alive with texture. Some smooth and glistening, others rough with cartilage or scaled like a fish from a waterless dimension. When they press against the walls, the paint bubbles and warps. The cabin's skin dissolves into the thing. It breathes in the timbers, a wet, rasping sigh vibrating through the floorboards.

Crack. Crack. Crack. Dozens of attackers recoil. Lotte's body bends. Her bones shatter and twist. Slits tear open on the sides of her body at the rib cage. More tentacles stretch down to the ground and lift the body. Her head and chest face upwards as six tentacles usher her towards me. A human spider contorted and hungry. Her head lowers, leaving her chin facing the ceiling. She watches me with upside down eyes. Her mouth wide, frozen in a silent scream. The creature scuttles towards me. My grip tightens around the knife. The other tendrils and tentacles watch. Thirsty for the battle.

Tentacles push against the ground and this new Lotte is airborne. There's no time to move. She tackles me to the ground. An unnatural tongue, long enough to reach my face, despite the backwards face, unspools and licks me from chin to forehead, leaving a syrupy pink residue.

I push the knife into the side of its head, resulting in dozens of screeches. Each tendril and tentacle joins the chorus and my bones ache from the volume of sound. The hunting knife meets no resistance in Lotte's head. No bone. No cartilage. Only soft tissue. Her corrupted body deflates.

What was once a living creature is now a skin blanket that covers my naked body, covering me in ooze and slime. Pulling it off is a struggle. It adheres to my body and refuses to let go. My skin becomes its skin. A wet shirt that refuses to leave its host. I slide the hunting knife between my body and the deflated monster and work it along my body like peeling an apple.

When it finally comes free, it drops to the floor with a plopping sound that makes me gag. My body is covered in the ick, but at least I'm free in time to see Pecan stand. His body contorts. Bones snap. Arms dangle like licorice. Tiny tendrils poke out of the bullet wounds that pepper his body. Little snakes sticking their heads out of the ground. I step over the flattened skin that used to be a drug mule, and ready myself for whatever this new Pecan has to offer.

Pecan's first step is wobbly. His legs don't seem confident in whatever has taken over his body. With each step, he may gain confidence. I need to get to him before he figures out how his new body works. I break into a sprint and tackle him before he can figure out the steering of his new vehicle.

I land on top of him and immediately feel the tug of his tendrils as they push against my exposed skin. His mouth opens, exposing his teeth, and he snaps them at me. I pull my head back in time to avoid being bitten.

His bullet wound tendrils are burrowing inside me. They push through the first layer of skin, seeking refuge in a new host.

I hold Pecan's head down and drive the hunting knife into his right eye socket. As it was with Lotte, there's no resistance. Only mush. Like pushing a butter knife into a bowl of day old mashed potatoes.

He howls and out of his mouth comes a torrent of pink spray. Maybe vomit. Maybe something from a distant realm. It's sweet and acidic. Like artificial sweeter filtered through a 9-volt battery. It stings my skin and singes my eyebrows. After what feels like thirty minutes, the flow stops, and Pecan deflates.

I don't have the strength for this.

But I have to save the world. It's the reason I exist.

My eyes search for another weapon.

One enormous appendage drops from the ceiling. Its tip split into dozens of smaller feelers. They probe the air, sticky threads latching onto the furniture. Lamps. Chairs.

Tables. It makes its way to my wrist. Each touch is electric, a slow horror of sensation. Slimy. Cold. Impossibly wet. My skin crawls, but I can't pull away; both adhesive and probing, intimate in a way that knots my stomach.

There's no other weapons. But in the kitchen is a bag full of pellets. And in those pellets is enough violet to give me the strength to turn this battle.

My knife swings wildly. Tendrils are discarded. They hit the floor and writhe like a headless snake.

I'm on my feet and barreling towards the kitchen. Tendril and tentacles bold enough to reach for me get amputated.

When I reach the bag of pellets, I waste no time. My fingers peel open the balloons and shovel the pills into my mouth. Dozens at a time.

A scream pierces the air. A sound not of this world. A screech that supplies its own echo. Mourning mixed with orgasm. It's primal. A bellow from a time before man.

With more pills in my mouth than I can possibly swallow, my tongue sets about sorting them to try and get them down in an orderly fashion. Like making sure all the 2nd graders get out during a fire drill.

Ve is up and charging. The crater in her face has been filled with a tentacle so long it drags on the floor between her legs, leaving a trail of pink goop.

With only half the pills swallowed, and the rest crowded in my cheeks, Ve's tentacle raises. And even from what has to be six feet away, it reaches me and wraps itself around my neck and body, pinning my arms to my side. Ve stands still, allowing the tentacle to coil back to her, with me inside it. It's grip tightening with every turn.

I hack at it with my knife, but air escapes me. All I want is to get a fresh dose of clean air, but this cabin has none to offer. My few gasps of breath produce nothing more than pollutants from some other dimension.

Suddenly, Ve and I are nose to nose. She stares at me like I'm in a cage. There's recognition in her eyes, but she has no memory of how she knows me.

Time fractures. It morphs and turns in impossible angles: a thousand eyes glinting along a sinewy mass. Mouths whisper in syllables my tongue cannot form, suckling against the wood. The cabin is no longer a cabin. It is a mouth. A maw. A body stretching its limbs into ours, with each pulse the floor bulges beneath us like wet clay.

My bones break as her tentacle tightens. The knife saws. But it's hard when the only range of motion is supplied by my wrist.

Air is a precious resource that I'm losing every second. My wrist burns from exertion and my hand goes numb. The knife clangs against the floor.

The only weapon I have left is my desperation.

And these pills in my mouth.

I bite down on her tentacle and pull off a chunk. Her body flinches from the pain, but I waste no time in covering the wound with my mouth. Whatever pills I have left in my cheek get spit into the tentacle through the opening.

The tentacle and whatever is flowing through it is sour and metallic. A mix of curdled milk and loose change. I don't know how many pills I ejected from my mouth into her, but her grip starts to loosen.

Her body must be absorbing the pills. I scramble for my knife. There's no telling what Fidget Electric will tell her to do.

Ve's face contorts. The tentacle withers and shrinks. Her body convulses, and soon she's melting. Pink steam rises from the goo as her body slowly decomposes from the bottom up, sinking into the floor. First her feet. Then her ankles. Then her knees and so on until the only thing left is a puddle of goo.

The cabin wails and pleads.

Tentacles stretch from all around and wrap themselves around me. I hack at what I can, but there's easily two dozen of them. I can't reach them all, and the ones I don't reach grab my legs. My arms. And my neck.

I try to scream, but the sound is swallowed in the slick suction of tentacles latching to my chest. I feel them tasting and memorizing. Stealing my thoughts. Pillaging my senses. Everything familiar dissolves: the chair, the floor, the smell of pine smoke. Only slime and suck. Wet muscles crooked at impossible angles creep closer to my face, probing my thoughts, my fear, my mind.

And then, as one final shudder passes through the cabin, the floor parts like curtains in a breeze. Outside, a world unfamiliar flickers in and out of eyes I'm not sure are mine. Tentacles pull me into an abyss bathed in light and charged with electricity. Cold brings a numb comfort.

Promises were made, but never kept.

Join My Newsletter

Want more? Join the community for deals and exclusives.

https://thedefpix.com/pages/connect

Author's Note

During eighth grade, my geometry teacher had to take some time off. I can't remember the exact reason, but we had a substitute teacher for the entire week. On Monday, before class started, she told us that if we behaved and got everything done we needed to do each day, she'd let us spend the last five minutes of class telling jokes.

Each day, Monday through Thursday, students told jokes for the last five minutes of class. On Friday, she told us it was her turn to tell us some jokes. Sure enough, we did everything we needed to do and we behaved ourselves. So for the last five minutes of class, the substitute teacher told us a couple of jokes.

One of the jokes she told was the joke I used in this book.

Eric Williford

May 2026

Atlanta, GA

ABOUT THE AUTHOR

Eric Williford grew up in Northern Virginia, where he spent his time playing sports and consuming late-night B movies. This love of Roger Corman, Troma, and exploitation films has seeped into all of his artistic endeavors.